Undead Ed

Undead Ed

RAZORBILL

Published by the Penguin Group
Penguin Young Readers Group
345 Hudson Street, New York, New York 10014, U.S.A.
Penguin Group (USA) Inc., 375 Hudson Street, New York, New York 10014, U.S.A.
Penguin Group (Canada), 90 Eglinton Avenue East, Suite 700, Toronto, Ontario,
Canada M4P 2Y3 (a division of Pearson Penguin Canada Inc.)
Penguin Books Ltd, 80 Strand, London WC2R 0RL, England
Penguin Ireland, 25 St Stephen's Green, Dublin 2, Ireland (a division of Penguin
Books Ltd)
Penguin Group (Australia), 250 Camberwell Road, Camberwell, Victoria 3124,
Australia (a division of Pearson Australia Group Pty Ltd)
Penguin Books India Pvt Ltd, 11 Community Centre, Panchsheel Park, New Delhi
– 110 017, India
Penguin Group (NZ), 67 Apollo Drive, Mairangi Bay, Auckland 1311, New Zealand
(a division of Pearson New Zealand Ltd)
Penguin Books (South Africa) (Pty) Ltd, 24 Sturdee Avenue, Rosebank, Johannes-
burg 2196, South Africa

Penguin Books Ltd, Registered Offices: 80 Strand, London WC2R 0RL, England

10 9 8 7 6 5 4 3 2 1

ISBN 978-1-59514-531-4

Library of Congress Cataloging-in-Publication Data is available

Printed in the United States of America

Undead Ed

Rotterly Ghoulstone

ILLUSTRATED BY

Nigel Baines

razOrbill

An Imprint of Penguin Group (USA) Inc.

LESSON 1: FIND A GOOD TEACHER

How I used to look →

My name is Ed Bagley ... and I might just be your best friend. You know why? I'll tell you. One day, the things that happened to me might just happen to you ... and, if they do, you're going to need some serious help. Well, here it is.

Forget everything you've ever seen or heard about werewolves, zombies, and vampires. Done that? Awesome—now, listen up... because I'm going to tell you the single most important fact you'll ever learn:

BEING UNDEAD SUCKS

...especially if you're a kid.

The three most miserable guys I know are *all* vampires, werewolves go insane *really* quickly, and ghouls cry all the time. Me? I'm a zombie . . . and that's no picnic. Of course, I didn't used to be like this. I used to be just like you: a normal boy from a normal school in a—well, okay—semi-normal town.

First things first—if you're going to learn anything about the undead, you need to grasp the three BIG rules:

1) Everything dies . . . not just your hamster. Dying is a natural part of life (unless, like me, you're hit by a massive truck on your thirteenth birthday—there's *nothing* natural about that). You live, you die. Get over it— I did.

2) Living people don't see or hear the dead. You know why? It's because they don't *want* to. *Nobody wants a corpse for a friend.* It's logic, really—you'd be the same way. If you don't believe me, ask yourself this simple question: if you were in a room with two other people and one of them was dead, which one would you talk to? Exactly. When you're oozing pus and slime from a lovely variety of flesh wounds, you'd be amazed how many people will look right through you.

3) The dead have their own problems. They can get upset, they can fight with each other, and, more importantly, they *can* die. Yeah, that's right—the dead can die. They just don't do it very often.

So ... I guess it's time to tell you my story. I'll go right back to the beginning so you can throw up in all the right places ...

LESSON 2:
KNOW YOURSELF

I live in a place called Mortlake. It's a fishing town, and most folks think it's hidden. In fact, it's as easy to find as any other town in the world, but people tend not to see things

WELCOME TO MORTLAKE

that upset them . . . and Mortlake upsets people. The dead run *riot* here—and I'm not kidding—the place is full of zombies, vampires, ghouls, werewolves, and all the other horrors you can think of. Trust me, if it oozes slime, eats flesh, drinks blood, or chomps on bone, there's a good chance it lives here. But I didn't know that when I was alive.

Mortlake is a real dump. There's a rumor that it became the way it is because, back in olden times, the people of Mortlake got into some sort of dispute with a band of local witches and the town was cursed. It's an easy story to believe. You can tell Mortlake is cursed just by standing on the cliff and looking down: it's all lopsided streets full of collapsing houses with crooked chimney stacks and no windows. If you want to make the place seem halfway normal, you have to stand on your head and squint.

I was thirteen years old on the day I died, and I'd lived in Mortlake all my life. I guess I was a wimpy kid: I once broke a rib by sneezing, and I'm pretty sure I'm the only person ever to cut themselves opening a packet of chips (they were salt and vinegar, too—that *really* hurt). Then there was the time I broke

an arm in gym class, waving at a pal—or even that morning in the science lab when I got savagely beaten by the teacher's four-year-old daughter who she'd brought from day care with a head cold.

I pretty much hated my life at school: everything except—well—except *her*. You know the one; I bet there's a her in your school too.

My "her" was called Candy Lipsnicki, and she was a femme geek—my buddies said that means a "girl nerd." I reckon I spent half my school life staring at her and the other half pretending I *wasn't* staring at her. Candy had a beautiful face: it wasn't the most beautiful face in the world, but I think it might have made the top hundred.

She had curly blond hair, green eyes, and a kind of odd squint that always made it look like she was about to ask a question.

Sadly, she never asked *me* anything, even on the day I brought a *Savage Sword of Kull* comic to school and I could see she was dying to look at it.

But back to my accidents. A year before I died . . . this is important and I'll explain more later if I've still got a jawbone . . . I electrocuted myself on the back of a carnival truck at the local circus. I was being an idiot, trying to get some kids from my school (including Candy) a free ride on the bumpers by jerking around with a control panel. All of a sudden there was a flash and a sizzle; the shock went right up my left arm and practically fried my brain.

I didn't actually die, but after the accident I would faint a lot: one minute I'd be walking along the street and the next I'd wake up back at home in bed. How creepy is that? The doctors told my folks it was a "psychological" problem, which means they didn't have a clue what was wrong. All I know is that I had really weird dreams afterward: running around in odd places and basically trying to kill myself in a million ways, always using my left hand. Rough, huh?

Well, it gets a lot worse...

LESSON 3: AVOID DYING (IF POSSIBLE)

There was a depot about half a mile from the edge of Mortlake. Apparently, it was a "distribution warehouse" for an Internet company, whatever that actually meant. The people of Mortlake *hated* the place...

...and that was because of the trucks.

No one really knew why they went so fast along Outskirts Road. It was like they filled up with rocket fuel instead of gasoline before they left the gas station. My best friend's mom always said that it was a miracle no one had been killed on the road, but the thing about miracles is that they tend to run out.

On the night I died, I was on Outskirts Road doing a school project on insect behavior. It was dark and stormy, and I was totally bored. My birthday had been the usual disaster: a big party where only five

of my friends turned up and three of them wandered off to "do something fun." Then I got a shard of paper birthday hat stuck in my eye. The party was such a bust that the rest of us went out to finish the school assignment instead.

Anyway, I decided to quit the project after a while and head to my best friend's house. He had a PS3 in every room because his dad got compensation after an accident at the morgue. Well, I *say* accident . . . but starting a frying-pan fire in a room full of dead people seems like stupidity to me.

So I headed off to see if he was home. Now here's where it gets a bit crazy. Just remember, if I lived it, you can read about it.

It was cold as well as wet and windy, so

I was totally hoofing it through the pouring rain. Then it happened.

Running across the widest part of the road, I suddenly felt the most incredible, crippling pain shoot up my left arm. At first, I thought maybe I'd been stung by a massive wasp, but then the pain got worse and worse and *worse*.

Unable to move my arm, I staggered slightly and made for the far side of the road. In doing so, I failed to look where I was going and stepped through a broken grate in the middle of the road. Yeah—*through* it.

MAJOR fail.

I doubled up in pain, twisted my foot, and

folded over like an old deck chair. As the sky emptied gallons of water on my head, I made everything worse by wriggling to get free—I jammed my ankle under the bars and wedged my shin between them and pulled what felt like a tendon in my *other* leg as I tried to wrench myself out.

It was no good—no matter which way I twisted and turned, my foot wouldn't work loose.

Then came the truck.

Don't worry, it all ends well, but in the moment it was definitely a bit messy. Looking back, I guess I did everything I could have done: I shouted out and waved my arms and stuff . . . but that massive eighteen-wheeler sure wasn't stopping. It hit me *head-on.*

I was thrown into the air, hit a tree, and cracked like an egg on the side of a frying pan.

Did I ever mention how much I hate truck drivers?

Anyway, I know all this because I *saw* it. There I was, drifting away from the scene like a very thin handkerchief blowing in the breeze, farther and farther until the road became a thin gray line and the trees melted into a shimmering sea of green. The world swam away and the lights of Mortlake all bled together . . .

LESSON 4:
TAKE CARE OF
YOUR BODY

When I woke up, I found myself lying in a stinking sewer. The whole place was glowing with a strange, yellow-green wash of light . . . which turned out to be coming from me. I was covered from head to toe in something that might have been mud but that I strongly suspected—due to the smell—was something worse.

I felt dead.

I had been . . . *decapitated.* I know: I saw it happen. I saw my own head rolling up the road:

I think it even knocked over a traffic cone. Yet here I was, full-headed—now that was weird. I've seen loads of movies where guys get beheaded, but I've never seen one where the head rolls back on again. I can't have dreamed it, surely?

Hmm . . . head working, no pain. Had it been . . . what . . . SEWN back on?

Euggghhhhh.

I tried to raise a hand to my throat, but it wouldn't budge. Nothing would. My muscles were frozen. I tried to blink, or sniff, or swallow but failed to get the slightest reaction from my body. All I could do was lie completely still with my eyes wedged open by some strange gunky stuff, observing the weirdest stage of my sad, pitiful existence.

Then . . . then something started to move.

My left arm, which was stretched out in front of me, twitched—once, twice, three times. After that, nothing happened for a few seconds.

I watched and waited . . . feeling *nothing*.

Then, with the speed of those very tiny ceiling spiders that leap when you try to

squash them, my left hand flipped over and all four fingers clawed into the slimy cracks on the sewer floor. They wriggled a bit, hooked themselves well into the cracks, and then flexed, dragging my body toward the edge of the weedy, scum-covered bank.

There was a problem: my legs were trapped under something. This was apparently bad news for my freak arm, especially since I was starting to get back some feeling in other parts of my body.

The fingers on my left hand flexed again, but this time they dug into the cracks with such frantic force that a soft and disgustingly sloppy ripping sound echoed around the sewer. To my horror, flesh and bone tore from my shoulder and my arm slapped noisily onto the wet stone. I gasped, partly because I was shocked that I was able to breathe *at all*, but mostly because a disgusting green ooze had begun to pump steadily from my now-empty shoulder socket.

A terrible stench filled the sewer.

My former arm flopped around like a fish gasping for air, then seemed to realize it was free and stuck up a thumb to celebrate.

As it scrambled farther and farther away from me, I managed to cry out—a pathetic, tiny little sound that barely escaped my lips.

"Hey," I managed, trying to get used to the sound of my own voice. "Hey! Arm? Arm! Come b-back . . ."

There was no reaction, but then, how could there be? It didn't have an ear!

Fingers working madly, the arm made a break for it, eventually toppling over the edge of the bank and sliding into the filthy sewer water below. It started to swim away, circling over and over in the water in what might have been a perfectly normal front crawl were it not for the fact that it was missing an entire body beneath it.

As I looked on, the arm disappeared under an archway and was gone. I think the sight of it vanishing might have shaken me from my frozen state because I finally managed to wriggle my legs free and struggle onto my feet, stumbling around in a sort of bewildered daze as the discharge from my open wound began to slow to a steady, sickening drip.

I raised my single remaining hand to my neck, expecting to feel a line of sharp stitches, but there was nothing. It was as if my head had somehow suckered its way back onto my neck. I gagged at the thought and almost threw up.

This was the start of my new life. I was undead . . . and it didn't just suck. It BLEW.

That being said, my previous existence hadn't exactly been perfect . . .

FLASHBACK INTERLUDE

GRIM LIFE EVENTS NO. 1
—HALLOWEEN

I said before that I never in my life spoke to Candy Lipsnicki, but that wasn't exactly true. I did speak to her ONCE . . . on Halloween.

It was the worst conversation EVER . . . and if it had been a scene in a movie, it would have run like this:

SCENE: Two kids arrive at the same door on Halloween: a boy in a skull mask and a girl in a rabbit costume with the face cut out. NIGHTMARE ELEMENT: The boy has his PARENTS with him (yeah, you read that right). Parents are both dressed smartly and neither of them is SMILING.

Boy presses bell. There's an eternal pause while they wait for the door to be answered by the old woman who lives there.

Boy: Heya.

Girl: Hey.

Boy: It's Candy, isn't it?

Girl: Yeah.

Boy: Cool; thought so. I've seen you around at school. My name's Ed Bagley. I'm in your class.

Girl: Oh.

Boy: I'm a skeleton. What are you supposed to be?

Girl: The Easter Bunny.

Boy: Is that a Halloween thing?

Girl: It's the way I do it.

Boy's FATHER: Ed would have come as a werewolf, but he needed the toilet really bad and he couldn't get the suit off quick enough.

Boy's MOTHER: So we had to wash it.

END.
OF.
MY.
LIFE.

What I've always wondered is this: why did it take that old woman so long to answer the door?

LESSON 5: GET YOURSELF MARKED

At the beginning of the week, I had written out a list of things to do before Friday night arrived. I thought I might spend a night or two completing Fortress 7 on Xbox, maybe catch up with a few buddies on Facebook, possibly even do Mr. Bixby's summer geography homework. One thing that wasn't on the list was "Die and spend Friday night chasing your own renegade arm through a stinking sewer system," but—list or no list—that box was seriously getting checked off.

I was belting it along. I never realized how fast I could run, despite the fact that (a) having only one arm majorly screws up your ability to run in a straight line, and (b) slipping in your own blood is a serious drawback for the newly undead.

The one thing I was seriously failing to outrun was my own stink. Back when I was alive, I might have been guilty of the odd smelly armpit or a few secret bits that only got a wash on the weekends, but now *everything* stank: my teeth, my hair, the backs of my hands. I could even smell my own *face* . . . and it was ripe.

"Arm!" I screamed, desperately looking for a manhole cover so I could figure out where the heck I was. "Arm! I know you're down here somewhere! You belong to me!

GET back here and face me like a—like a *man's* arm!"

An eerie, almost demonic cackle echoed through the sewer. It gave me shivers up what was left of my spine.

Then I saw the note.

It was pinned to a drainpipe and dripping in what appeared to be some sort of black mucus. The writing looked like blood, but I couldn't be sure. I snatched at it almost on instinct and felt a sickness rising in my stomach as I read the words:

Hellllo, Loser,

It's me—your left hand. You can probably tell—nobody else spells Hellllo with four l's. Get ready for a dark surprise, Ed . . . because I've been waiting for this moment for YEARS.

On the day you electrocuted yourself, all those moons ago, I woke up and found myself inhabiting your pathetic stringy limb. I've been fighting for control ever since. Remember that scaffolding accident when you were twelve? I did that on purpose. You probably don't remember, but I actually slapped you on the back of the head after you fell. You see, I've always had the feeling that I'd be free if I ever managed to kill you, Ed, and—as it turns out—I was right.

I wrote you this letter because I felt you twitching and I wanted to gloat. How or why you're back from the dead, I don't know—but I DO know I'll kill you if I ever run into you again.

Got any problems with all that? TALK TO THE HAND!

I froze, and the note slipped out of my shaking fingers. What *was* all this madness? What had I done to deserve *any* of this?

I caught sight of my reflection in the shimmering glow of the drainpipe and almost threw up. I looked like a road accident, which I guess I should have expected since technically I *was* one. I felt sick and hungry. I knew I had to forget my traitorous arm for the time being and get out of the sewer—and fast.

When you're dead, you think exactly the same way as you did when you were alive, so my first instinct on finding myself in a strange place like this was just to go home.

But you can't go home when you're dead. Ever.

I didn't know that then, so I tried to do it anyway. But as I began to hunt through the maze of tunnels for a way out, I ran into something right out of a horror movie, something that made *me* look like a little fairy princess . . .

I heard the growl before I saw the outline of the thing that had made it. If I'd seen the face first, I might have added my own stink to the sewer.

There, crouched slightly above me on a metal scaffold beneath an open manhole cover, was a moving shape covered in patchy brown fur.

I froze and gulped some fetid air.

"Hello?"

"Grrrrraaaaaaaaaaaaaaaargh."

The snarl that came from the creature was the most wild, feral noise I'd ever heard.

I swallowed a few times. "Look, I think I might have died, and my arm's gone off and—"

I took a step back as the creature dropped onto the sewer floor, peeling apart its lips to reveal a mouth full of giant teeth and thick, dripping gums.

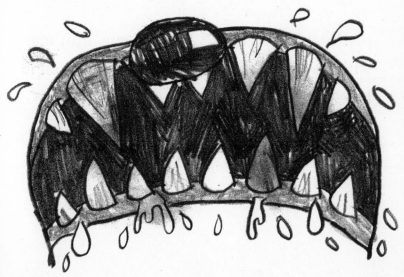

"Grrrrrrrrrrrrrrrraaaaarggggghh."

"The thing is . . . um . . ."

As the beast crouched, ready to spring, I turned and ran as fast as my stiff, undead legs would carry me, down tunnel after tunnel after tunnel, twisting left, turning right, leaping pipes, and ducking walkways. I could hear the *thing* behind me at every step, galloping forward on all fours, moving like a racehorse as it sniffed and slobbered, hunting me down.

When it caught me, I was taken off my feet with such force that I felt like a pin hit with a bowling ball. I hurtled to the ground in a furious ball of teeth and claws and screamed like a banshee when the crazed beast bit a massive chunk from my leg.

My flesh still hanging in its terrible jaws, I flailed around with my single remaining arm, snatched up a loose piece of pipe from the sewer floor, and scrambled until I managed to reach the creature. Then, with every last ounce of strength I could muster, I brought the pipe down hard across the creature's twisted, mangy skull.

"Yiiiiiiiargghgghghghghghgghghghghh!"

The cry echoed throughout the sewer, a frantic, petrifying, canine howl of pain that pierced my ears.

The pipe was fiercely snatched from my grasp and a voice said, "What on earth do you think you're doing, meathead? Are you nuts?"

My instinct made me look around for the source of the voice. Almost as a last resort, my searching eyes came to rest on the still-ravenous face of my attacker.

"D-did you speak?" I gasped, ready to try for the pipe again.

The beast nodded. "Yes! What's wrong with you? Why did you hit me in the face with this?"

I scrambled back onto my feet . . . which took longer than I'd hoped.

"M-me? What *are* you? You just, like, *seriously* attacked me!"

Astonishingly, the beast seemed to relax a bit.

"I'm Max Moon," it said. "I'm a registered werewolf, and I'm your assigned DB . . . er . . . that stands for Dead Buddy. I attacked you so you wouldn't get eaten. Sorry about the growling thing—I'm a bit of a joker."

I stood in the half-dark for a few seconds, looking down at my new wounds and trying to work this all out.

"You ate some of my leg so that no one else . . . er . . . eats me?"

Max shrugged.

"I didn't *eat* your leg—I bit you to leave my mark. Trust me, it helps if you've got a wolf mark—keeps all the other wolves at bay. You'll be okay with the vampires since they don't touch zombies. Anyway, biting you seems to have taken that green glow away, but don't bother to thank me or anything . . ."

With that, he turned and began to lope off—I had to run at full speed just to keep up with him. As we hurtled along in the murky sewer, I was filled to bursting with questions for Max, and they all came tumbling out. Things like "Where are we?" and "What do I eat?" came a close second to the more pressing ones like "Have you seen my evil arm?" and "Wait up—I'm a ZOMBIE?"

LESSON 6:
KNOWING WHEN
TO RUN

Max didn't answer *any* of my questions. In fact, he almost completely ignored me as we moved faster and faster through the sewer.

It was only when we reached a heavy metal door cleverly concealed behind a section of fake pipe work that he turned around, very slowly, and bared those horrific teeth again.

"I want you to listen to what I say now, *very* carefully . . . and I don't want you to say anything until I'm finished. Understand?"

I nodded, grateful for the attention.

"First, you stink worse than my last dump of the day—but that's because you're effectively a rotting corpse . . . and it's not your fault. We'll get you some air freshener, which should take off the edge—okay?"

"Er . . . yeah?"

COUGH SPLUTTER

"Good—glad that's cleared up. Now, see this door? It leads to the Undergraves: that's the name we give to the maze of tunnels beneath Mortlake Cemetery."

"We're still in Mortlake?"

"I'll ignore that. Now, we're going to run quite quickly . . . and if you see a fat baby, I want you to leap onto my back and hold on tight with your one arm."

"Wait a minute—a fat baby?"

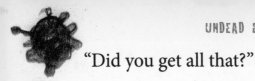

"Did you get all that?"

"Yeah, but seriously—"

"Just do as you're told and we'll both be fine."

As Max turned to wrench at the door with his hairy hands, I wondered—and not for the first time—if he was actually insane. First he'd bitten off half my leg and now he was telling me to watch out for fat babies? Had I seriously landed the world's only lunatic Dead Buddy?

The door flew open and Max started to run. I tried to keep up with him once again, and we both hurried through the weird, earthy passageways. I noticed that there were holes above us at regular intervals. My stomach turned over as I thought of all the dead people who'd been stashed over our heads, lying there in ancient coffins, crumbling to dust in the—

A little blur flashed across a tunnel section behind us. I heard it before I saw it and spun around to see if I could fix my gaze on the shape. No good—it had vanished completely.

Not wanting to bother Max, I continued to follow him down several new passages, but I was looking over my shoulder the whole time, wondering if I might be going a bit nuts myself.

Is my deranged arm coming after us? Could it be that—

The flash appeared again, only this time it slowed to a blur, scrambling along the walls and ceiling with such incredible speed that I almost bit my tongue as I jumped out of my skin in shock.

"Fat baby!" I screamed. "FAT BABY!"

I catapulted myself onto Max's back and he took off like a rogue missile. Within seconds, we were bombing it along the tunnels so fast that I could hear my hair ripping sparks from the roof. I risked a quick glance back and soon wished I hadn't.

"Faster!" I yelled at Max. "There're hundreds of them! It's a fat baby army!"

The description was actually pretty accurate—the things following us looked exactly like newborn babies, albeit extremely overweight ones with glaring eyes and rows of razor-sharp teeth.

That was when Max truly furred up. While I was still clinging frantically to his back, his bones began to crack and expand, twisting and turning under all the flesh and the hair so it looked as though he was spawning an alien or something. As I desperately tried to keep hold of him, he morphed from a two-legged wolfman into a giant, rampaging canine monster . . . and he started to move at a speed that made my teeth ache.

Unfortunately, the fat babies were just as fast. As we shot along each new tunnel in a maddening blur, the little critters were snapping, biting, and shearing tiny scraps of flesh from my back and Max's ankles. I could feel every near-bite, every sharp pinch as those needle teeth missed their mark by a fraction of an inch. I closed my eyes and prayed—then realized I was dead anyway so praying probably wasn't much use.

Then, all of a sudden, everything changed. There was a breathtaking rush of air, a stomach-churning, gut-thrusting leap upward, and I felt the outside air hit my face in a cold gust.

We were slowing to a careful sprint. There were gravestones all around us and the full moon was high in the sky. The familiar sight of Mortlake spread out below us, and I breathed an audible sigh of relief when I realized I could no longer feel the nail-biting terror of being followed.

Max padded to a halt and half-dropped, half-dumped me on a fresh grave.

"Those things," he panted, morphing back into a sort of hairy teenage tramp, "are ghouls. Try to avoid them if you can—they eat the dead." He saw the look on my face and added, "Yeah, I know they look like fat babies. Pretty gross, huh? They tunnel into new graves from below and devour the corpses. I hate 'em. Oh, welcome home, by the way!" He grinned wolfishly and pointed at the gravestone behind me. "I can give you a few minutes if you want—some folks find this part . . . um . . . hard to deal with."

I nodded vacantly and turned to look at the message carved on the stone. It said:

ED BAGLEY
BELOVED
SON AND BROTHER
JANUARY 25, 1999
JANUARY 25, 2012

LESSON 7:
ASK A LOT OF
QUESTIONS

I looked at the gravestone and back at Max. I guessed I should have cried or at least felt something . . . but the only thing clouding my head was the buildup of questions that all desperately needed answering.

I scrambled off the dirt of my own grave and struggled to my feet. It was like doing a one-armed push-up, but eventually I managed it.

"I was *buried*?"

Max nodded.

"B-but how could I have been? Surely, I *just* died."

Max peered around him, then up at the moon. He sniffed the air—once, twice, three times before staring back at me with a suddenly wary look in his eyes. He seemed distracted by something, *something that scared him*. It was a while before he spoke again.

"You died last Monday, Ed. Your mangled body was found at the scene and sewn back together for the burial, which was on Friday. You would probably still be in your grave, but you died while under a powerful curse . . . so you're back. Sorry, dude, but it's true—your possessed arm clawed its way, towing you, into the tunnels after a bunch of ghouls came to eat you. Um. . .you were still unconscious while all that was happening, which was probably for the best."

"But . . . my arm—"

"Ripped six ghouls into shreds, yeah. That's why I've been watching you for so long—I was waiting for it to detach before I came to get you. No way I'm messing with that *thing*." Max stared at my empty arm socket and, for a few seconds, looked as though he was about

to tell me something important. Then he seemed to change his mind. "Look, you have questions, Ed—I get that—but I'm lousy at explaining stuff to people. You really need to speak to the leader of our . . . er . . . gang."

"You have a gang?"

"Yeah. Sort of."

I tried to do as I was told and keep quiet, but I just couldn't hold back the tide of curiosity welling up inside me. "I am a zombie, though? You told me that much! Are zombies . . . er . . . a bit pathetic?"

Max shrugged. "Not always. It's all ups and downs, you know. Being undead sucks."

An icy wind had blown up from the coast

road, and I was surprised to find myself feeling cold. It got slightly more chilly, however, when part of my face fell off.

"What on earth?" I looked down at a small section of my own bloodied cheek, which looked a bit like a piece of jelly on the ground.

PLOP

"Get used to that," Max warned. "It's likely to happen a lot—just let it go. Don't try to stick it back on or anything. The parts that fall off of their own accord tend to smell worse than the parts that hold on."

"So what happens now?" I asked, trying not to get tearful as a whiff of my own stink almost made me gag. I would have hugged myself for comfort, but—with just one arm—what was the point?

Max motioned for me to climb onto his back once more.

"We need to get to Mortlake Middle School by sunrise."

"The school? *My* school? B-but what if someone I know—"

"The living don't see or hear the dead," he said as I clambered onto his back and prepared myself. "We can see and hear *them*, but it's like background static—you know, weird shapes and sounds."

"Like ghosts?"

"Exactly. Now, just hold on—we're going through the trees—it's safer that way. If anything major falls off, give a shout and I'll double back."

I clamped on tight. We started off at a decent pace, and the air began to rush through my stringy, undead hair.

57

LESSON 8:
HIDE WELL

Max Moon could smell danger a mile off. Unfortunately, his way of dealing with that sense of danger seemed to be to stop without *any* warning and dump me unceremoniously in the dirt.

I hit the ground while still in the position of holding onto Max's back and bounced along like a basketball until I hit a tree. When I eventually rolled to a halt, I checked myself for more missing bits, but the only bad development seemed to involve my right eye leaking some sort of pus that smelled like a cross between peanut butter and dog turds.

"Eugghh!" I moaned.

"Shh! Shut up, will you!"

Max was crouching on his haunches between the trees, sniffing the air and scraping up some turf with his bare feet.

I hope he's not going to take a dump, I thought. *I wouldn't know where to look . . .*

Fortunately, Max quickly lowered himself onto his stomach and put one ear to the ground instead.

"We need to get into the trees," he growled. "It's coming."

Leaping up, he dug his powerful claws into the bark and shinnied up it. For a few seconds, I genuinely thought he'd just left me there. Then there was some movement from the lower branches and a furry hand appeared.

"Here, take hold!"

I reached up and Max pulled me into the

tree. We climbed a bit farther and both slithered onto the highest branch overlooking the path through the wood.

"What are we hiding from?" I whispered.

Max rolled his eyes. "What do you think?"

I didn't hear any noise, but looking down, I could see something moving through the shadows.

Max signaled for silence by raising a hairy finger to his lips, and we both held our breath as my hand appeared on the path.

It still looked like nothing more than a severed arm, but there *was* a sort of demonic confidence in the way the fingers spider-climbed along, dragging the limb after them.

The arm worked its way underneath the trees but stopped when it reached ours and began to rise like a snake, balancing on the hand.

I looked up at Max, but he was frozen with fear.

We both lay deadly still, willing the evil terror below to shrink away, but it didn't.

The arm stayed exactly where it was for several long minutes.

Then it flopped over again and crawled away, every bit as quickly as it had arrived.

"Awesome," Max whispered. "It's going the wrong way!"

I smiled with equal relief and was about to jump back down from the tree when Max snatched hold of me and held me back. "Wait!"

There was a low rumble, and a line of earth began to spew out of the ground. It ran all the way along the path, as if a team of particularly determined moles was tunneling beneath it.

The line ran out of the woods and seemed to trail after the arm.

Finally, Max jumped out of the tree, landing easily. Sadly, he had to catch me when I tried and failed to do the same.

"The ghouls?" I hazarded, dropping to my knees and scooping up some dirt. "I don't understand—why would they follow my arm?"

Max blew out a heavy breath. "Ghouls become servants to anything that frightens them," he said. "They have a pack mentality."

"And my arm is now top dog?"

"Yeah. It looks that way." Max turned to me with a very serious expression on his face. "Now, come on. We've got to get into town . . . and that means facing an enemy every bit as dangerous as the ghouls and—sadly—a lot more intelligent."

LESSON 9:
LET OTHER PEOPLE
DO THE TALKING

I saw the danger before we got anywhere near the boundary of Mortlake. Three shadowy, shifting shapes detached themselves from the first few buildings on the coast road and floated toward us.

"Every dead zone has border guardians that keep out intruders," Max explained. "They're called wraiths—and you don't mess with them unless you have to."

I nodded.

The wraiths approached. They reminded me of a bunch of kids wrapped up in their parents' dusty bedsheets, but I knew they were deep trouble by the way Max tensed up as soon as they came into view.

"Let me do the talking," Max growled, fur beginning to spring from his face and arms. "That way, at least you might get to keep your three *remaining* limbs."

"Are they undead too?" I asked, my own hair bristling to back up the statement.

"Uh-huh," said Max grimly. "The kind that nobody likes."

As if aware of our fears, the three strangers immediately grounded themselves, grew long, spindly legs, and started advancing toward us

in a shallow, awkward series of movements that made them look like puppets on the stage of a twisted theater.

Max padded to a halt and I climbed off him just as he furred up completely. He'd gone for the half-man, half-dog thing this time, bipedal with dripping fangs. He looked mean.

I waited for the things to approach, thrusting my hand into a tattered pocket to stop it from shaking.

There was definitely going to be a fight. Max *hadn't stopped* mutating. The fur around his face seemed to tighten into a flurry of tiny needles and his hands turned into ravening claws of death. His bone structure changed too, his gums thickening to make room for the sprout of new teeth he was forming along the back of the existing ones.

I looked down at my empty arm socket and my weedy, tattered body but decided to man up and look hard anyway. I even spat on the ground, just to show I was ready for a dustup. Sadly, it didn't work because a good third of my tongue hit the ground along with the spit. I guess it was the effort that counted. I was determined to show no fear, but—in truth—I was so scared I could probably have turned and run right at that second. Still, I wasn't going to let *them* know that.

The figures stopped their progress about five feet away from us, and the lead one sprouted a sickly-sweet smile that revealed just as many teeth as Max now had cramming his own gum line.

"He'sssss not coming in," it said, thrusting a needle-thin fingernail into Max's chest. "He'sssss too dangerousssss."

Me? Dangerous? In what universe, exactly?

"You're not allowed to stop us," said Max with a snarl. "Jemini got permission from Evil Clive."

This announcement seemed to cause the three figures some sort of odd amusement, and the two at the back began to shiver in a way that suggested they might even be laughing.

"It knowssss where he is allll the time," said the leader, quite firmly. "If we let him in . . . it will follow."

The arm, I thought. *They're talking about my arm.*

When Max didn't reply, I stepped forward, very carefully. "What if I promise to just stay out of everyone's way and not cause any troub—"

I never finished the sentence. The wraith came for me in a blinding burst of speed, but Max was there to meet it.

The werewolf shot forward and cannoned into the shrouded figure, which swiftly burst into flame and began to fight back. The other two flared up just as quickly, arms and legs rotting away as the fires licked up and down their bodies. One flew directly into the sky, screaming a sort of high-pitched whine, while the other—

to my complete horror—made directly for me, bellowing with arcane fury.

I ran like a six-year-old girl in the opposite direction.

However, as I tried to put as much ground as possible between myself and the wraith, I did risk a glance back toward Max . . . and soon wished I hadn't.

To this day, I've never in my life (or death) seen a fight quite like it.

The blazing creature punched Max repeatedly in the face with a fistful of flaming fury, sending up charred, smoldering tufts of fur and casting a million tiny embers into the air with each assault. All the while, it screamed like a stray hyena hollering for its mother.

Max, meanwhile, employed a mouthful of killer canines and two sets of razor claws to carve heavy, sickening lumps of flesh from the body of the beast. It was like watching some sort of demon barber going at a bad hairdo with lightning speed.

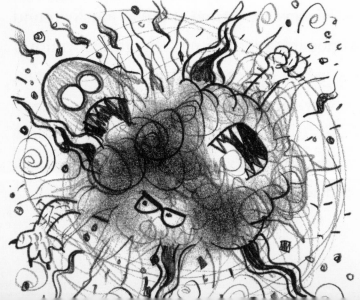

There was so much blood, flesh, and chaos that if you narrowed your eyes, the scene became a kaleidoscope of red and white flashes. It was absolutely, mind-meltingly disgusting.

Thankfully, I was otherwise occupied . . . and I continued to run like a tiny frightened spaniel at a dog-kicking contest. The *thing* was hard on my heels.

"Can't we just talk about this?" I yelled, putting on an extra burst of speed. "You might get to like me if you'd just give me five minutes to—arrgghhh!"

I felt a sharp pain in my ankle, and it caused me to leap forward at an even greater pace. I ended up running around in an ever-wider circle, making my way back toward Max . . .

... who was in big trouble. Max's fight was *not* going well. For every chunk the werewolf ripped out of his opponent, the wraith grew an immediate replacement. It must have been like fighting a video-game baddie with unlimited lives. To make matters worse, the fiery punches and kicks quickly took their toll on Max, who was seemingly caught in a deeply instinctual and feral fear of the flames. He was losing the fight and howling in pain with every new attack. At length, he gave one last bestial cry and collapsed.

My *one* friend had been defeated, and he was a total monster. What chance did *I* have?

I ran back toward the town, glancing over one shoulder to see the figure still in hot pursuit. Now it was *deadly* close. Burning fingers suddenly fastened onto my shoulder, lifting me off the ground and into the air.

"Leave Mortlake," said the rasping voice. "We will not asssssssk you again."

I looked down at the wraith, only just noticing that the flaming grip wasn't actually burning my tattered skin.

The creature gave a vile hiss, and a forked tongue darted out of its slit-like mouth. Then it twisted around and hurled me the length—the entire *length*—of the field on the edge of town. I flew past the back of the grocery store, the garage, the hair salon, and even the town hall before hitting the church gates so hard that they exploded in a shower of splintered wood. I slammed onto the concrete steps that bordered the church, and the gatehouse roof came down on top of me. All in all, it was a violent and terrible attack that would have killed the world's strongest man about twenty times over.

I felt . . . nothing.

I just sniffed and struggled to get up, pushing back the rubble of wood and rocks in my path. Sadly, I didn't possess supernatural strength, so it took ages for me to break free. Still, it was the first time in my entire, miserable existence that I'd ever gotten up from a fight. I couldn't believe this was happening to me—I was finally . . .

. . . a bit of a punk.

The wraith watched with a strangely irritated expression as I clambered over the last of the debris and marched back toward it.

This time, I went straight on the attack, leaping at the creature and screaming a battle cry that I'd heard in a fantasy movie when I was eleven years old. It sort of went, "Yargargarga!" I think.

It worked well. The wraith drew back at first, as if expecting some major onslaught, but when I simply gave it a sharp slap across its right ear, it took umbrage and went absolutely *dynamite* insane.

Screaming madly, it snatched me off the ground by my feet and began to spin around and around in wide, arcing circles. I think I might have actually fainted at one point, possibly due to the rush of air, because I don't remember exactly *what* happened when it let go. I recall a greenish sort of hazy blur and after that nothing until I hit the church roof and took out the bell known in Mortlake as Ten Ton Tom. I landed on the far side of the church, broke two gravestones on the way down, and made a hole in the ground that would have taken six men hours to dig.

Then I got up again, dusted myself off, and hurried around to the front of the church.

Wow, I was even *running* faster than usual—my legs might be rotting away, but there were at least a couple of muscles down there now. I was fighting the flab!

The wraiths had not only regrouped on the road into town, they had also doubled in number. Now there were lines of them! Reinforcements had been called by the one that had floated into the sky.

Max was staggering back toward me, looking like a ragged imitation of a really *insane* hellhound. At least he was alive—ish.

"Nice try," he panted, blood dripping off him. "But it's no good—we won't get past them unless we get more help. Give me a few seconds to get my breath, and I'll give the call . . ."

I nodded, still shaking, and looked down at

my ravaged body. The green glow around me had vanished, but I still looked like the special in a butcher's shop window. In fact, my rapid journey through the church wall had taken off almost an entire layer of skin.

I was about to remark on this when Max gave the most explosive, earsplitting howl I've ever heard in my life . . .

LESSON 10: NEVER TURN DOWN A FREE HAND

When Max eventually stopped howling, it was like all sound had been removed from the world. I couldn't even hear my own pulse, but that was probably because I didn't have one.

Then, from all over the rooftops of Mortlake in every direction, came a series of responding howls—some soft and sad, a few fierce and maddening.

"More werewolves?" I hazarded, feeling stupid for asking the question. After all, it was hardly likely to be a horde of killer hamsters, was it?

Max nodded. "Rogue ones," he growled. "Let's just hope they don't attack *us*."

I boggled at him. "There's a chance of that? Aren't they your friends?"

"Are you crazy? I wouldn't call my own pack into a fight they couldn't win! I gave a wounded cry instead—the rogue wolves will come to feed on me. Still, it's definitely worth—ON THE GROUND! NOW!"

Max hit the grass, dragging me off my feet.

"Argh!"

My chin had barely grazed the first blade

of grass when something black and shiny flew past our heads. It looked like some sort of demonic spear as it arced through the air and plowed directly into the muddle of wraiths congregating on the edge of the town. There was a muffled cry, then a scream. The first wraith exploded into a hail of green flames and burned up in the air.

Max and I glanced at each other, but our attention was quickly diverted back to the scene, where the *thing* had seemingly scampered from one wraith to another and was doing an equally grim job on its new victim. Within seconds, the edge of town was a chaotic fusion of tortured screams and billowing sheets wreathed in green flame. I was so scared by the sight, I almost swallowed my own tongue.

"Wha . . . is it?" I managed.

Max was straining to see. He'd craned his head over the grass but looked too scared to move any closer.

"It's your lunatic arm!" he whispered, nearly frantic himself. "It's killing them all!"

My eyes nearly popped out of their sockets.

"What! How?"

"I don't know! It's tearing them up or something! I've never seen *anything* take out a wraith before! EVER."

There were several more of the crazy, whining screams . . . and then silence.

"Oh no!" Max whispered. "It's standing on top of the fence like a cobra! It's going to see us!"

I reached up with my own remaining arm and dragged him down until he was lying flat next to me.

"It can't *see* anything," I said, trying to forget that the arm had torn apart a pack of ghouls. "It's just an *arm*."

Max looked like a frightened puppy now—all his hair had withdrawn and he was shaking like a leaf. "It's *your* arm," he whimpered. "What does it want?"

I shrugged, trying to keep calm . . . but Max was getting more stressed out by the second.

To make matters worse, the earth started to churn up around us, arcing a line directly toward the fight.

"The ghouls!" I whispered, clawing at Max's leg. "We've got to get out of here—it's all going to kick off!"

Max looked down at me. "I don't know why *you're* panicking," he snapped. "It's not going to attack *you*, is it?"

I thought about what to tell him for a moment and then decided on the truth.

"I think it might," I said. "It did threaten to kill me if it ever ran into me again."

"You could have *told* me that!"

Everything had gone quiet.

Max risked another glance over the top of the grass.

"Has it gone?" I ventured.

He shook his head. "Nope—standing stock-still. I tell you, that thing totally freaks me out. It's even twitching . . . oh no—that's *gross*!"

"What?" I was about to sneak another peek at my evil arm when I realized that Max was looking at *me*.

"Your face! Worm! WORM!"

I quickly raised my hand to my left cheek and found both a newly opened hole and something slimy wriggling in it.

"Ugh!"

I pulled the twisty thing from my face and tossed it aside. We both watched it wriggle away. I'm not sure what smelled worse: the worm or whatever it had left in my cheek.

"Dude." Max shook his head. "That's sick."

I returned my attention to the town road, where the ghouls were now erupting all around the arm like a little pack of loyal puppies. The sight sent a shudder right through me.

I was about to suggest to Max that we both carefully creep away when the werewolf pack arrived.

Then total chaos erupted . . . everywhere.

LESSON 11: LEARN TO MOVE FASTER THAN OTHER FOOD

Max had taken off at the speed of light, only this time he hadn't bothered to drag me after him. I had to run at what for me was break-neck speed even to keep him in view. Behind us, a cacophony of howls, whines, and ripping limbs indicated that the werewolves had run straight into my evil arm and weren't doing a whole lot better than the wraiths.

As we skirted the town in a wild arc, leaping low walls and short fences and moving along the backs of the narrow fishing cottages that made up the fringe of Mortlake, I saw Max begin to slow. It was just as well—I'd lost part of my foot as I cleared someone's flower border and wasn't really left with much solid bone to run on. In fact, I'd actually doubled back to get some of the toes that had gone AWOL, and I had them in my pocket. I didn't want to let go of the important stuff, you know.

Eventually, Max trotted to a halt, glancing at me with an almost-casual indifference as

I arrived next to him, almost *literally* falling apart with exhaustion.

"I th-thought you were supposed to be my Dead Buddy," I panted.

Max gave me a guilty grin. "Sorry about that. We werewolves have a saying: you have to move faster than other food."

"Nice."

He flashed another canine smile. "There's not much in this corpse yard of a town that scares me, but your arm is like—well, put it this way: I doubt the pack will last too long against it. If I had to make a bet, I would put money on there being a lot of werewolf soup for the ghouls tonight."

"Sorry," I said, feeling it was somehow necessary to apologize for my rogue limb even though I had no actual control over it. "I wish there was something I could do . . ."

Max sniffed the air again and seemed to relax slightly.

"Forget it," he said. "Let's just make for the school so you can get some answers. You must be, like, totally lost by all this stuff."

"A bit."

Max nodded, and we began to head for the distant outline of Mortlake Middle School.

As we walked along, a sudden memory flashed inside my mind. *Max told the wraiths that I'm their new member . . . and he said two names.*

"Who is Jemini?" I asked.

Max turned to look at me. "She's a vampire," he said. "I think you'll like her: she's second in command of our group."

"And Evil Clive is the leader?"

"Yeah."

"Odd name—Evil Clive. Is he actually, er, evil?"

Max whistled between his teeth and I definitely noticed him tensing up.

"Oh yeah," he said. "You really have to earn his respect. Some folks think he's the devil . . . but I reckon he's just, like, well—you know— twisted beyond words."

Great, I thought. *Sounds like a really nice guy. Can't wait to meet him.*

LESSON 12:
FIND SOME
WEIRD FRIENDS

Mortlake Middle School's tiny parking lot was deserted as Max and I crunched up the gravel toward the main building. I knew the place well, since I had gone there every day. At first, it looked as though nothing had changed. Then Max reached through the broken pane of glass on the front door and pulled it open . . .

. . . and I saw the display.

The flowers.

The cards.

The photographs of me.

This was insane. I wasn't even popular at school—I was bullied every single day of my life.

"Best not to dwell on it," said Max sullenly. "Let's just get inside."

The stench in the foyer was absolutely gut-wrenching, but I soon realized that it was coming from my hair and not from the rotting cat corpse I expected to find behind the reception desk. Apparently, undead dandruff smelled a lot like gerbil vomit.

I marched into the main corridor behind my strange new friend and found myself trying to guess where we were headed. I couldn't.

We passed the English Department and pro-
ceeded through Geography, Languages, and
even beyond the gym.

Where would the undead hang out? I
thought. *Surely not in the History Department? That would just be rubbing it in!*

Imagine my surprise when Max finally
opened a door that led into the science lab. I
was even more shocked when the lab turned
out to be packed *full* of deadies. It was like a
scene from your worst nightmare. There was a
little clique of pale, thin kids perched on top of
a bench beside the tank containing Mr. Phelps's
pet axolotl. They were all good-looking in a
bloodless sort of way, so my immediate guess
was vampires. Opposite them was a group of
scruffy, hairy skater boys covered in tattoos.

"My other wolf brothers," Max confirmed, but I wouldn't have needed to ask. They all smelled terrible. "Don't take their expressions to heart—they're *always* angry."

In fact, everyone in the room was staring at me, and not in a good way. The werewolves growled and gave me searching glances until Max's mark was indicated by one near the front, while the vampires looked surprised that I was there at all.

I noticed, with great unease, that there were no other zombies.

"Just ignore everybody here," Max muttered as every head turned to watch us proceeding down the middle of the room. "Everybody except *her*."

Standing at the far end of the lab was a tall, dark-haired girl with lots of freckles and a stern but slightly unfocused expression.

"That's Jemini," Max whispered. "Watch out for the mood swings."

The girl didn't smile until we were practically on top of her, and even then it looked like a real effort.

"You must be Ed Bagley," she said. "I'm Jemini Yaddle. Welcome to Mortlake Middle School."

I've been here a million times, I thought. However, out loud I said, "Thanks."

"Evil Clive will see you in a few minutes," she said, pointing at a door where the lab assistants hung out. "He's with someone at the moment." She turned back to me and tried for another fake smile, but it twisted awkwardly and looked in danger of turning her face inside out. It was fairly obvious she wasn't the full ticket, but I couldn't quite see why.

"Before you go in," she managed, wiping the corner of one watery eye, "I'd like to ask you a big, BIG favor on behalf of the entire company."

As she spoke, every vampire and werewolf in the room crowded in around me.

"Your arm is something of a problem. It savaged the wraiths, mauled a group of rogue werewolves on the outskirts of town, and I wouldn't dream of sending my vampires to fight something so destructive. Instead, we've decided to band together and lay a trap for it up at the depot. We think we know how to stop it, but we'd like you to act as the bait."

My face froze as if I'd just been slapped. *Hard.*

"You want me to—"

"Act as bait, yes. It is *your* arm, after all . . . and *your* responsibility. If my teeth suddenly jumped out of my mouth and went roaming around biting people, then it would be *me* responsible for sorting it out. That's only fair. Am I right?"

I smiled weakly and—noting that Max said nothing—gave a reluctant nod.

"Sure," I said.

After all, it's only an arm—what's the worst it could do?

I swallowed, trying to block out the image of screaming wraiths and slaughtered were-wolves.

The door to the lab assistant room suddenly creaked open, and a small boy came out sobbing and clutching at his face.

Jemini watched him collapse on the floor in a trembling heap before giving me the first genuine smile I'd seen.

"Evil Clive will see you now," she said.

108

LESSON 13: WHEN YOU'RE AMONG KOOKS, ACT LIKE ONE

I felt myself shaking quite violently as I approached the door. There was nothing but shadows all around the opening, and I couldn't help glancing back at the poor wretch who'd just staggered out of the room.

I reached out and gingerly pushed back the door, stepping inside and coughing a bit to announce my presence. Something jumped in my throat, but since it was likely to be one or more of my tonsils giving up, I decided to ignore it.

There was no reply from the gloomy depths of the room, but to my horror, I could see a skeletal hand resting on top of a desk beyond the solitary alcove in the far corner. There was a chair positioned in front of it.

I closed the door behind me and swallowed.

"Er . . . hello?"

Nothing. I couldn't stop Max's description of Evil Clive from rumbling through my head: *You really have to earn his respect . . . some folks think he's the devil . . . twisted beyond words.*

Then something inside me snapped. *I'm a member of the undead now—I need to start acting like it.*

Taking a deep breath, I strode across the room and spun around as I arrived before the alcove, sliding into the chair with as much cool style as I could muster.

"I'm Ed Bagley," I said . . . and froze.

Sitting before me was a grinning human skeleton in a ripped baseball cap with "Deaf Donkey" scrawled across the front in neon-yellow ink.

I waited a few long and incredibly awkward seconds, my eyes wide with shock,

before staring around the room and firing off a question to anyone who might be hiding in the shadows.

"Um . . . is this some kind of joke?"

There was no reply, and the amount of conversation coming from the lab outside told me that absolutely no one was playing a practical joke.

I turned back to the skeleton, which hadn't moved an inch.

"Are you Clive?" I asked, feeling like a complete idiot. "Um . . . how's it going? It must be really difficult, running an undead gang like this."

Silence.

He's totally dead, I thought. *I mean, sure— so am I . . . but this guy looks like he's about three hundred years past his use-by date. Are they all CRAZY?*

I looked down and noticed a folder open in front of Clive. It had my name on it.

Feeling ever so slightly guilty for not giv- ing Clive *respect*, I snatched the folder, spun it around, and began to investigate the contents.

There was a single sheet of paper inside, containing a series of bullet-point facts. I read:

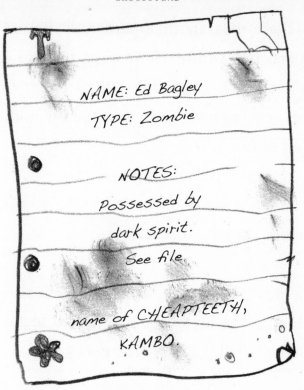

NAME: Ed Bagley

TYPE: Zombie

NOTES:

Possessed by

dark spirit.

See file

name of CHEAPTEETH,

KAMBO.

I stared at the page until the lines blurred into a single, smudgy mess.

Possessed? Are they talking about my arm? Who in the name of sanity is Kambo Cheapteeth?

There was another paragraph below the report, but I didn't have time to read it. A knock on the door shook me from my reverie, and I quickly re-positioned the folder in front of Evil Clive.

I turned just as a worried-looking vampire hurried into the room.

"Sorry to interrupt," he said. "But something's come up, and I really need to talk to the boss. It's . . . it's an emergency."

I nodded, quickly got up from the chair, and started to walk away, but I simply *had* to listen to the conversation as I left.

"Clive," said the vampire. "We're going to arrange an ambush for the zombie's arm, and—"

He suddenly stopped as if he'd been interrupted. Then he said, "What? Oh yeah—of course. I think we'll . . . Yeah—up at the factory, just before dawn. Do you think that . . . Of course! Right, I'll be sure to check it out."

Yep. Crazy, I thought. *They're all absolutely crazy.*

But I'm definitely not an idiot, and I quickly decided that I needed to fit in with this ragged band of deadies—after all, they were basically my *only* friends in this strange and depressing new world I was now condemned to wander.

Thinking on my feet, I began to curl up my lips and *make* myself cry. Bursting through the door, I staggered into the waiting crowd and collapsed onto my knees.

SUPERB ACTING

"He's EVIL!" I cried. "He's soooo evil!"

There was a general murmur of agreement from the gang, and suddenly I knew I was *in*.

When I eventually managed to "pull myself together," I found that both Jemini and Max were treating me with far greater respect.

"He can be very nasty when you first meet him," the vampire girl admitted, putting her arm around my shoulders and shaking her head sadly. "He had me in tears several times. I'd never met anyone with such a horrible temper."

He had you in tears, I thought. *Why? Did his skull roll onto your foot or something?*

"I know people who'd throw themselves out of buildings rather than talk to Clive," Max said seriously. "He can just give you that *look* and you KNOW you're in deep trouble."

"You can say that again." I nodded, wiping a fake tear from my eye. "Look, guys, thanks for trying to make me feel better." I smiled weakly, now convinced that they were both several cards short of a full deck. "I really appreciate it."

"It's time to go," said a voice. "Everyone is ready."

I turned around to see that the lab was now packed *full* of deadies. There were five vampires and six werewolves, all furring up with fangs ablaze and demonic fires glinting in their eyes. There was also a very small, miserable-looking boy in pajamas holding a teddy bear, who seemed completely out of place in the room. However, since no one else made any comment, I thought it best to keep quiet and just ignore him.

Max slapped me hard on the back.

"You up for this, Ed?"

"Er . . . yeah. I guess so."

"Great. Let's go take out your freaky arm!"

LESSON 14:
NEVER BITE OFF
MORE THAN YOU
CAN CHEW

We all piled into a convoy of fat monster trucks the vampires had brought along, which was something of a surprise. I still couldn't really understand how the living couldn't see and hear us, especially if we were all ripping each other to shreds, screaming, or slamming around in off-road vehicles. However, there was still so much about this place that I didn't understand . . . like how the most dangerous undead creature in Mortlake was apparently the thing I used to scratch my leg with when I got an itch. It just didn't add up.

To make matters worse, Max had climbed into one of the other trucks, leaving me alone with the moody vampire Jemini and the small boy I'd seen in the lab earlier. The werewolf was driving and the rest of us were bouncing around in the back.

"I'm sorry if I seem a bit harsh," Jemini said. "But you *do s*mell like a six-year-old chicken leg, and besides, I'm still trying to get past my *own* death. Dying was . . . *very* traumatic for me."

"Yeah," I said. "It probably is for most people, though."

She looked doubtful and possibly on the verge of tears.

Wow, I thought. *Mood Swing City.*

"I don't think I'm quite over it yet," she went on. "Dying, I mean. Did you know I drowned?"

"No."

"Well, I did. One day, I will tell you all about my extraordinary death, but now . . . now isn't the time."

"I drowned too," said a voice. I looked down at the boy. This time, I *couldn't* ignore him.

He really was *very* small, with dark hair and a squint. He couldn't be more than four or five years old and was surrounded by an eerie, milky-white haze.

"Hello," I said. "I'm Ed. Ed Bagley."

He looked up at me.

"I'm Forgoth the Cursed," he said, holding

up the exceedingly peculiar-looking teddy bear. "And this is Mumps."

"Forgoth *the Cursed*?"

"Yeah, it's an awesome name, isn't it?"

"Totally. Um . . . how did you become cursed?"

Forgoth sniffed. "I was possessed by a devil intent on the destruction of my immortal soul," he said, as if he was reading a set of cooking instructions. "It was a major bummer."

I whistled between my teeth.

"So aren't you frightened of tagging along with us? You know, fighting a demonic hand and all?"

Forgoth shook his head.

"Naaah," he muttered. "Mumps protects me from most stuff."

I looked down at the ragged stuffed toy. "You *are* talking about that teddy bear, right?"

Forgoth grinned. "Oh, Mumps isn't a teddy bear," he said. "He's a Free-Roaming Demonic Entity."

And that was it. He didn't say another word.

The trucks all skidded to a halt outside the depot. I'd been there a few times before, when the school was doing a project in it, but to be honest, the place always gave me the creeps.

There was a massive sign over the doors that read: CINFAX DISTRIBUTION WAREHOUSE— MORTLAKE DEPOT. The grounds outside were littered with cardboard boxes and absolutely *crammed* with trucks: low loaders, moving trucks, even a few eighteen-wheelers. I wondered if the one that hit me was there.

"Okay, everyone," said Jemini, jumping down from the first truck as the entire gang began to shuffle around her. She put her hand into the pocket of her jeans and pulled out a long glass vial containing some green liquid. "Evil Clive has given us this: it's a mutating fluid that will turn Ed's evil arm into some-thing a bit more humanoid and therefore much easier to fight."

There was a sort of half cheer from the gang, which died away when Jemini walked over to me and thrust the vial into *my* hand.

"Um . . . ?" I managed. "You want *me* to splash this over my arm?"

"You catch on quick," she said, putting her head on one side and smiling that sickly-sweet smile. Then she turned back to the gang. "Everyone else HIDE! Now! We attack just as soon as Ed's completed his part of the assault."

And that was it: in five seconds, the entire

gang had vanished. They were literally *nowhere* to be seen. I stood alone in the parking area of the distribution depot, surrounded by abandoned trucks and old cardboard boxes. I felt small, pathetic, and hopelessly lost . . .

. . . and I didn't have the slightest clue what I was supposed to do.

So I just stood there.

After a few minutes, I looked down at the vial of green liquid in my hand. It was bubbling.

Then I heard the noise and looked up again.

A truck was coming up the road—a big one. It was moving at a decent speed and heading straight for the factory.

Inside the truck, which veered all over the road in every direction, the human driver was sitting on the front seat, fixated on the disaster unfolding in front of him. My severed hand was clamped firmly on his head, gently tapping a finger on one side of the man's skull when it wanted him to skid left or right. Every time it tightened its grip, it appeared that the poor driver's foot would slam down on the accelerator, urging the truck to reach greater and greater speeds as it hurtled up the road.

Never one to be caught twice with the same death, I quickly came to my senses and leaped out of the way, just in time to see the truck plow into the vehicles behind me. I watched in frank astonishment as the giant cab crunched in on itself, dragging its trailer behind it. I caught a glimpse of something that made my stomach turn somersaults: the driver, his leg crushed, fell out of the cab, dragged himself onto his other foot, and staggered toward me, the hand still clamped on his head.

Eyes rolled back and jaw sagging, his mouth began to move as if he was being controlled by a deranged puppet master.

"Ed! I'm coming for you, Ed!"

I could probably have run forward at that point and attacked him. I could have stood my ground and said something like, "Bring it on, slackjaw!" However, I didn't do any of those things.

Nope. Instead, I did my roadrunner impression again.

I didn't even reach the tree line.

The arm catapulted itself from the head of the poor trucker and flew *over* the top of me, landing squarely on the tarmac and blocking my path.

It reared up again, just as it had done in the cemetery, and a terrible mouth tore open in the palm of the hand.

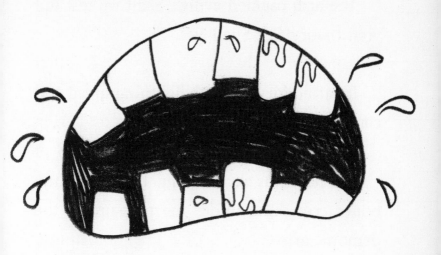

"This is the end for you, Ed," it growled. "I should have finished you off in the sewer."

I had nowhere to run and nowhere to hide. I felt my hand tighten on the vial. Suddenly, I was very, *very* angry.

"Why *didn't* you finish me off in the sewer?" I snapped. "I think it's because you can't. For some reason, you need me alive . . ."

The arm cackled evilly. "Shall we test out your theory, Ed? Shall we?"

It darted forward with lightning speed and clamped hold of my face.

The pain was excruciating. I could feel my bones crunching under the pressure of the demonic grip.

"Arggghhh!"

"You like that, Ed? Do you? DO YOU?"

I heard one of my cheekbones crack. I snatched hold of the arm with my own hand and tried to wrench it free.

I managed it, but the lunatic limb then clamped hold of my right leg and ripped a massive lump of flesh from the thigh. It was *biting* me with savage little teeth.

"Arggghghh!"

I collapsed onto the ground, writhing around as I tried to shake off the demented appendage.

"Help!" I screamed. "Somebody help me!"

However, the hidden deadies were either too scared or too selfish to come to my aid. I was completely on my own.

The arm finished chomping on my flesh and swapped legs. It was about to take an even bigger bite from my left calf when I made the only offensive move I could think of.

I swung around with my remaining arm and smashed the vial over my crazed attacker. The glass exploded and green liquid spurted all over the place. I quickly rolled out of the way, shedding my shirt when some of the vial's contents splashed onto it.

The arm was not so lucky. It was absolutely CAKED in the emerald grunge, from shoulder wound to fingertips. I had done my job well.

Suddenly, the parking area exploded with vampires and werewolves, crowding in on every side. While the arm flopped around on the tarmac like a fish out of water, I scrambled onto my feet.

The vampires had all grown elongated fangs that now hung down over their lips and made them look deadly. The werewolves were in wolf form, padding around the arm with snarls and snapping fury.

Two things happened very quickly.

First, the arm began to mutate.

Then, the tarmac erupted.

Still thrusting myself backward, I screamed out loud when the ground between my legs spewed upward in a volcano of dirt and tar-mac. A ghoul appeared, its eyes glowing with malicious hunger and its little mouth already salivating at the thought of devouring my undead flesh.

I booted it hard in the face, but that just made it angry.

"Fat babies!" someone screamed. Ghouls sprang up all over the parking area, latching onto vampires and werewolves as a terrible fight began.

Everywhere I looked, vampires were rising into the air, biting into the necks of some ghouls while trying to shake off hordes of others. The werewolves were doing the same, shaking violently as if they'd just emerged from the sea and were frantically trying to get dry. Ghouls were flying off in all directions but scrambling back so fast that they were almost a blur.

Learn to move faster than other food.

I peered around, looking for an escape route. Max Moon and Jemini were fighting back-to-back; Max had one dead-looking ghoul hanging from his jaws while the vampire girl was sucking a gallon of blood from two more.

"Hold on, Ed," Max cried. "I'm coming to help you! Just hold on!"

But Evil Clive's gang was losing. Big time.

I finally found my feet and began to run *away* from the depot. Behind me, I heard a demonic voice in hot pursuit.

"Come back here, Ed—I haven't finished with you yet! Mwaahaaha!"

I glanced over my shoulder and saw—to my horror—that far from being destroyed or shrunk away, my arm had actually *lengthened*.

It was now a grotesque fleshy snake, and the hand had . . . *nine fingers.*

"Argghh!" I screamed as my twisted nemesis piggybacked onto a flock of ghouls in order to keep up with me.

I panted to a halt, completely out of energy, and turned to face my fate. Then I remembered that I wasn't that old, wussy, no-courage Ed anymore—now I was Big Ed. Zombie Ed. UNDEAD Ed.

"Hahahaa! You can't run, Ed!" said the tiny, mocking mouth. "You can never escape me!"

"He won't need to," said a small voice behind me.

Forgoth the Cursed took several quick steps

forward, threw his teddy bear between me and the arm's rampant ghoul horde, and screamed, "Mumps, Mumps, come out of the dumps!"

There was a strange popping sound, like someone piercing a bubble in a piece of bubble wrap . . . and then the ragged little teddy bear started to transform.

To this day, I can barely describe the thing that Mumps turned into . . . but what

I do remember—very clearly—is that it was like the gates of the underworld opened and spewed out something even a half-starved mongrel would leave on the edge of its bowl.

Mumps swept forward, a big, red, all-engulfing octopus with tentacles spraying out in every direction. As the ghouls did whatever they could to avoid the main body of the beast, Mumps collided with an oak tree at the side of the road, its horns impaling the bark

and rooting it to the spot. Quickly realizing it was stuck, the Free-Roaming Demonic Entity then struck out with seven tentacles, snatching ghouls into the air and flinging them off in every direction.

All the time, Forgoth the Cursed stood dejectedly in the middle of the road and watched the scene with a mixture of boredom and grim anticipation. Evidently, he'd sent Mumps into battle a *lot*.

I stood frozen to the spot, but that turned out to be a big mistake.

The arm appeared from nowhere, snaking around my shoulders and snatching hold of my throat with its nine spider-like fingers.

I cried out in pain once again as I felt the tiny teeth tear into my neck.

This time, my own desperate fury overtook my fear. I dug down deep, snatching up all of my newfound courage, and I got . . . really . . . ANGRY. I slapped my hand over *the* hand and dug my fingernails hard into the back of it. Then, still unable to release the grip, I lifted up the arm and *bit* it with all my might.

The grip released slightly and I wrenched the arm away, throwing it onto the ground. It cackled demonically and flipped over, the fingers working madly to send it crawling after me once again.

I was swinging on the end of my last nerve, and I had not an ounce of strength left in me. My only weapon against the arm now was knowledge . . . and I had far too little of that.

"Kambo Cheapteeth," I screamed, pointing at my grim enemy as it writhed toward me.

The arm stopped instantly. At first, I thought the words might have killed it, like some powerful spell taking mastery over an evil spirit. Instead, the arm slowly turned over and raised itself up once again.

Even in the silence, I could feel its surprise. I was about to shout again when Mumps came galumphing up behind the arm, snatched it out of the ground, and flung it with incredible force over the tree line.

I watched as my erstwhile limb flew high, high into the air. I didn't see where it landed, but I knew in my heart that this battle was far from over.

The arm would return . . . and now its mouthy hand had more fingers to fight with.

LESSON 15: EXPECT THE UNEXPECTED

I wish I'd hung around to find out whether the gang won its fight against the ghouls. I wish I'd taken more of a heroic stand against the evil arm myself. Unfortunately, I didn't. Instead, I did what I do best.

I ran.

But this time, it was different.

I ran with anger.

I ran with determination.

I ran . . . with a purpose.

Admittedly, much of the purpose seemed to involve keeping my jaw attached to the rest of my head. It had slackened considerably and I was terrified of losing it. To make matters worse, a horrible, tooth-rotting smell had started wafting up from my mouth to my nose, and I was praying it didn't have anything to do with another worm. Where did they come from, exactly? How did they get *in*?

Moving at high speed along Outskirts Road, I pounded the ground as if the very hounds of Hades were after me and as if my life (if I'd had one) depended on escaping them.

There were still two wraiths on guard outside Mortlake, but something about my expression and the speed I was going obviously stopped them from attacking.

I bombed it into the dark, deserted town square, past my old house, past the pizza parlor where my dad and I used to get my dinner on Friday nights, past the barber's where I always seemed to get the worst haircut in school.

School.

I sprinted up the drive, slammed through the double doors and cannoned along the corridors, past the English Department, past PE, Geography, and History . . .

. . . and into Science Lab 1.

There I slowed, a new determination in my eyes.

The writing at the bottom of the fact sheet in my folder. It must have said something more about me, maybe something about Kambo Cheapteeth? I needed to know.

I pushed open the door to Evil Clive's office and marched inside.

Naturally, the gang's inanimate leader was still in the same position, poised over my crummy folder with that stupid baseball cap still perched on his head.

"All right, Clive," I said sarcastically, snatching up the folder and dragging the sheet from inside. My eyes moved to the tiny paragraph below the heavy print. It read:

```
Ed Bagley is an inno-
cent kid who needs to find
peace. Save him from that
thing . . . if you can.
```

I felt my eyes welling up with tears, and the anger inside me was like molten lava in my stomach. My life, my *death*—it was all so unfair.

"Who *are* you, Kambo Cheapteeth?" I said to the world in general. "And what did I ever do to you?"

I turned to leave the room, but a skeletal hand suddenly closed around my wrist.

"Kambo was a circus clown," said Evil Clive with a grin. "And you *really* messed up his death . . ."

LESSON 16: FLASHBACKS CAN BE USEFUL

Okay, folks, I've held off on telling you this bit for too long. It's a horrible story, and I don't even like to remember it myself…but here goes:

FLASHBACK INTERLUDE
GRIM LIFE EVENTS NO. 2
—CARNIVAL CHAOS

On the dark and stormy night I had my carnival "accident," a lot of other stuff was happening that I couldn't possibly have known about. It was a bit like those horrible movies where fate makes five or six people run into each other at the worst-possible time.

Of course, I didn't know that then.

I was doing something dangerous and stupid, and—when you're a kid—that means you get blamed for pretty much anything else that happens afterward, even . . . even if it's not your fault . . .

. . . even if it would have happened anyway, and it was just your *timing* that sucked.

The rain was hammering down and we were all soaked to the skin.

I'd been trying to impress the cool kids in school, and that included Candy Lipsnicki. Not that she would ever have acknowledged that I was even alive, not after that awkward Halloween encounter . . . but I had to try. I remember how the two older guys who were with her laughed when I said I could turn the bumper cars on for them. They snickered at me, both of them, said the circus was shut, said *no* kid would have the guts to break into the truck and power everything up.

I said I wouldn't need to: the panel was on the *outside*.

I'd been there two nights before, with my mom and dad—I'd seen the guy in the sweats punching buttons on the back of the truck, the part connected up to the little kiosk where everyone stood in line and paid their money.

All the switches were labeled—it should have been the easiest thing in the world.

It wasn't.

I remember all of them watching me: the two goofy idiots from the estate and, most importantly, Candy.

I had to climb a bit, but it wasn't difficult. The panel was just a bit too high for me to reach from the ground.

Looking back, I don't even remember that much after my hands grabbed the sides of the panel.

All I know for sure is that there was a blinding flash and it felt like my whole body exploded.

I was told afterward that I'd been thrown back from the truck and had hit the ground, hard, and that my hair and fingertips were burned and smoking.

The two guys from school had run off; the girl called an ambulance on her cell.

When my parents came to the hospital, they went *nuts*.

When I got back to school, I was ignored by my so-called friends and mocked by the two rumor-spreading losers who ran off and left me.

I was *that stupid kid who electrocuted himself.*

The only person who actually spoke to me during those horrible weeks was the girl I'd been trying to impress. Candy told me that she felt sorry for me, that she should have stopped me from doing such a dumb thing.

She also told me something really odd, something that made me shudder, something I always thought of as being the worst coincidence in the world.

She told me that at the exact moment I put both hands on the panel, the truck got hit by lightning.

LESSON 17: LEARN ABOUT "UNFINISHED BUSINESS"

So that was how it happened, but I didn't have time to focus on the past for long. I shook myself from my daydreams and tried to remember where I was.

When the skeletal hand snatched hold of me, I almost jumped OUT of my skin.

Sure, I'd been frightened before—a million times. On balance, though, I don't think I've ever actually achieved *flight* in the same way

I did when Evil Clive sprang to terrible, animated life.

"What on earth!" I screamed, checking to make sure I hadn't filled my tattered trousers with a gallon of pee. 'Y-y-you're n-n-not r-real!"

"I'm your worst nightmare, kid!" said the scratchy, demonic voice. "Your WORST nightmare! Mwaahaha! Arghgh!"

The skeleton shot forward until its hideous grin was mere inches from my face.

I screamed. I was shaking like a leaf in the wind, but Evil Clive kept on coming.

"Are you scared?" he taunted. "ARE you? ARE YOUUUUU? ARRREEE YOU?"

"Yes! YES! YEEESSSS!"

"Good! I'll rip you apart, boy—I'll rip you APART!"

"Please!" I managed through trembling lips. "W-w-hy would you—"

"I don't *need* a reason—I'm Evil Clive! Arghgh!"

I closed my eyes and waited for the icy fingers of pain to find me . . . but nothing happened.

When I opened my eyes again, Evil Clive was sitting down at the table, writing on a piece of paper. Rather oddly, he'd turned his baseball cap around so that the brim was facing backward.

"Er . . ." I said awkwardly. "I thought you were going to rip me apart?"

Clive sniffed and looked up at me.

"Decided against it," he said, his ever-permanent grin fixed on my terrified face. "Bad for business. Sit down, will you? You're making the place look untidy."

I found the seat and very carefully lowered myself into it, keeping my eyes on the newly animated creature before me.

"You never moved when I came in before," I muttered. "You never said a single word."

Clive shrugged. "I was asleep. Besides, you've got bigger problems to worry about than me, boy—you'd better believe that."

I gulped some air and clasped my hands together to stop them from shaking.

"Kambo Cheapteeth is . . . in my arm? How?"

Clive sat back in his chair and steepled his skeletal fingers.

"I'll let you in on a little secret," he said. "Us deadies don't hang around for long. We're only here on personal errands—something folks call 'Unfinished Business.' I have mine, you have yours—the only difference with me is that I'm sort of a guide. My Unfinished Business is to know what everybody else's is and help them to solve it. I can't go to my rest until *all* my people find theirs. You are one of my people—get me?"

I nodded, but there was something I *didn't* understand.

"How did—"

"Kambo Cheapteeth was a clown, but he was also part of something called the Brotherhood of the Secret Smile. There were three of them, all circus performers, and every one was twisted—they were all quite, quite mad. They made the pact together—they'd all kill themselves at an appointed time on the night of the full moon; it was a dark ritual they named 'The Lightning Caller.' Kambo *summoned* the lightning that struck him in the back of that truck . . . the truck you electrocuted yourself on at exactly the *same moment*. His spirit passed *into* your arm."

My heart began to pound. I'd been walking around living my *life* with the dark ghost of an evil clown inhabiting my left arm.

How in the name of sanity could I not notice something like that?

Evil Clive suddenly stood up, accompanied by an orchestra of teeth-shattering clicks.

"I have band practice across town," he said, snatching up a trench coat from the back of his chair and putting it on.

Band practice?

I tried not to stare, but I couldn't help it.

The sight of a grinning human skeleton in a trench coat goes beyond odd and into the extremely surreal. I felt like I was in the twi-light zone.

"Before you ask," Clive went on, "destroy-ing Kambo Cheapteeth is *not* your Unfinished Business . . . but *his* UB may well be to finish *you*. After all, you ruined his death—there's a good chance he'll never catch up with his bonkers friends now . . ."

Clive strode over to the door.

"You have to finish this," he muttered, his bony fingers fastening on the wooden handle. "Come find me when you're done. Oh, and Ed?"

"Yes?"

"Be careful. You're not impossible to destroy—always remember that."

LESSON 18:
FACE YOUR FEARS
HEAD-ON

When you have no idea what you're doing, go with your instincts—they're pretty much all you can rely on.

I found myself walking back along Outskirts Road, heading for the factory.

I'd run away from my friends. In my fear and anger, I had deserted them. Was that who I was now? A guy who ran away at the first sign of danger? Was I really—in death—no better than I'd always been when I was alive? A sniveling, wretched freaky little coward who shrank into corners of the world and watched other people fight for me?

NO.

NO MORE.

NOT NOW.

NOT EVER.

As I made the decision to fight, it felt as though a weight lifted from my shoulders. I wasn't frightened anymore—not of the ghouls, not of the hand, and not even of the twisted soul of Kambo Cheapteeth. It was payback time—and I was going to be the one paying. I just needed to figure out how.

I walked along, sidestepping the multitude of corpses strewn across the road at regular intervals. There seemed to be an even mix of vampires, werewolves, and ghouls. Had all of these creatures finished their Unfinished Business? If not, could they really be dead?

I shuddered and continued trudging up the road. There was no sign of Forgoth or Mumps, and a feeling of deep foreboding settled over me. A storm was brewing, and I definitely didn't want to get electrocuted again . . .

"Hey."

I glanced over at a massive horse chestnut tree beside the road. Max Moon was sitting underneath it.

"Your hand didn't get you, then . . ."

Max was halfway between his (mostly) human form and that of the full wolf, but he was badly wounded. A sizable slash yawned in his side, and both his legs had been savaged.

"I'm really sorry," I said, hurrying up to him and crouching down. "This is all my fault—is there anything I can do?"

Max smiled, but the pain showed on his face.

"It was Jemini's plan, not yours," he muttered. "And we should have been ready for the ghouls. We weren't." He struggled to straighten himself up. "I self-heal; we all do. Even those corpses on the roadside will probably rise up again, but it takes time. I'm probably not going to be any use to you until at least—"

"No." I spoke firmly and looked Max directly in the eyes. "You folks have already helped me enough—this fight is one I really have to win on my own."

Max didn't argue. I don't think he had the strength.

I walked the rest of the way in silence.

When I reached the factory courtyard, I came upon a scene that looked like the set of a horror movie massacre. The enormous shape of Mumps covered much of the ground, and Forgoth sat atop his pet, looking miserable but far from grief stricken.

I self-heal, Max had told me. *We all do.*

There were wounded ghouls *everywhere*, but no sign of—

"You're back," said a voice.

I turned to see Jemini emerge from the side door of the factory, followed by a gang of injured but formidable-looking vampires.

"Your hand didn't come back," she said. "But I doubt it's dead. We need to lay another tr—"

"No more traps." I shook my head. "It's like I just told Max—I need to sort out my own problems, and if that means killing Kambo Cheapteeth all over again, then so be it. I just wanted to pop by and say thank you."

I held out my remaining hand, and Jemini looked down at it for a long time before she took it and we shook on our new friendship.

"Where are you going?" she asked.

I smiled grimly. "I'm pretty sure I know where my rogue limb is heading . . . so I'm going to go meet it. You know, in a guns-at-dawn sort of way."

The vampire girl smiled, and I noticed for the first time that she had braces fitted *over* the top of her fangs.

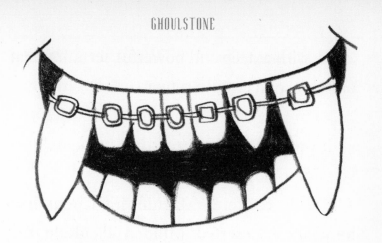

"Good luck," she said.

I nodded. "Thanks—if I don't come back in the next few hours, I'll be down a really deep hole or something."

With that, I turned and walked away, leaving all my undead friends behind me.

I felt sure that my arm was going to exactly the same destination to which I was now heading. Despite not having the slightest clue what my own Unfinished Business might be, I knew with a deep and powerful certainty that only one of us would return.

It was my arm or me.

Carble & Stein's Magnificent Circus had long since deserted Midden Field on the northern borders of Mortlake, but the ground remained a burned and desolate wilderness.

I remember the local council trying to clear the area after the circus had left, with little success. The grass stopped growing and a wild assortment of ugly crows seemed to congregate there, making horrible cawing noises and generally frightening off any other form of wildlife that wandered onto the abandoned ground.

I never knew about the death of Kambo

Cheapteeth or his creepy friends after the circus left, but I *did* know that the local kids never went up onto that ground—EVER.

The field was shrouded in a strange, thick mist as I clambered over the south fence and headed for the place where I knew that truck had been parked.

I didn't have flashbacks, not as such, but I could still vividly remember those two gawkers all standing around me as I lay on the ground, shaking and twitching with shock. One of them laughed—Candy cried—the other one just stared down at me as if I was dead.

The recollection sent a shiver up my spine as I came to a standstill on the very spot where I'd been electrocuted just over a year ago.

The hand was waiting for me in a little circle of grass that the heavy mists were giving a wide berth—they meandered around the edge of the tiny space but didn't seem to actually seep into it.

A possessed hand with nine fingers.

NINE.

It looked mutated beyond belief, like a giant spider awaiting its prey. It reminded me of the face hugger in the Alien movies, minus the tail.

I stopped and felt every muscle in my body tensing up.

"I don't think you *can* kill me, Kambo Cheapteeth," I said, clenching my fist. "But I really want my arm back, so I guess you're going to have to try."

I charged forward and my evil limb sprang into the air to meet me. Neither of us screamed, me because I wouldn't and my arm because it couldn't—apparently the mouth it had employed earlier was now sealed up and withered . . .

We collided in mid-air like two ancient warriors of legend. The hand went straight for my face and I made a grab for the socket end of the arm.

imagine this in super slow motion!

There was a dull thud as we hit the tough grass, me spitting, dribbling, and biting and the hand snatching, scratching, and clawing.

I felt the strength of its grip—the sheer, inhuman, brutal power that had rent the

ghouls limb from limb while I lay unconscious in my grave.

At the same time, I gripped with all my
might, my own fingers digging into the flesh
of the socket and my few muscles bulging and
straining as I fought to tear the limb away
from its rabid assault.

"It's . . . my . . . arm!" I screamed, rolling
over and driving a knee into the arm to help

me with leverage. "I want . . . it . . . BACK! Arghghgh!"

I swear I could hear my jaw beginning to crack under the terrible pressure of the evil hand's death grip.

Then I realized my one true advantage in the fight and I let my body go limp.

The hand smothered me and forced me onto the ground as I let the strength bleed out of my body. Then it took hold of my hair and rammed my head hard into the ground. Apparently assuming that I was suitably unconscious, it climbed, spider-like, onto the top of my head and gripped my skull with all nine of its fingers.

Then I felt the burrowing—a searing invasion of malign energy as the soul of Kambo Cheapteeth tried to get into my mind.

But that was the point.

It was *my* mind . . .

. . . and it was also *my* arm.

I sprang awake with a deep, guttural roar, focusing all my mental energy on the spirit and all my physical energy on the arm.

It wriggled like an angry snake as I snatched hold of the socket end, but I was fighting with a new strength and determination.

I might still be Ed Bagley, but I was also Undead Ed, zombie—a creature of darkness and purpose.

"Kambo Cheapteeth," I said, spitting through gritted teeth as I wrestled my enemy into submission. "This is *my* arm . . . and I want it back!"

Screaming with rage, I rammed the arm socket into my shoulder wound. A terrible light exploded from the fingers and ran along the length of the arm's flesh; it seeped out and buzzed all around the clearing.

The arm twisted madly to escape, but the ragged tendrils from my devastated shoulder were already twining and blending with those from the socket wound on the scabby appendage.

Kambo Cheapteeth was losing.

I was forcing him *out*—the corrupt mutations, the demonic mouth that still yelped and twisted in the palm, the dark soul that writhed beneath it.

My shoulder flesh knotted together and, with a final blazing flash of light, I was thrown backward, bodily, on to the dirt.

There was a sudden burst of thunder and a flash of forked lightning that seemed to come from *me* instead of the thunderheads floating above the field.

I rolled over and forced myself up onto my hands and knees, staring with a mixture of shock and pride at my newly re-joined arm.

Sure, it was a bit freakish-looking ... but at least it was my own. Well, most of it.

I waggled the fingers—all nine of them.

Then a horrible sensation of spine-tingling terror made me turn around.

LESSON 19:
NEVER GO IT
ALONE

There, standing on the grass about ten feet away in a baggy, hideously distorted outfit, was Kambo Cheapteeth.

The clown was about six feet tall, and it is difficult to know how to begin describing him. A mop of curly green hair stood out in the moonlight, but it looked as if it had been colored with green gloss that had burned up in too much direct sunlight. The hair itself was matted, and much of it stood out in darker swathes. Facially, Kambo was a monster—

bulging, bloodshot eyes and a plastic, blood-red nose overshot a mouth crammed full of rotting teeth and distorted gums. When he smiled, it was like the gates of the underworld opening to greet you.

"Thanks for forcin' me out, kid," the rotting teeth chattered. "I sheem to 'ave me ol' body back 'n' all. I can shtand, I can talk, I can move. I can KILL. I feel . . . pow'ful."

Kambo staggered a little way toward me, but there was a slight shimmer around his outline—it wasn't something I'd seen before, but it was something I instantly recognized.

"You're a ghost," I said, barely concealing my delight. "Ha ha! Bad luck, CHEAP-TEETH—you lose."

Kambo looked down at himself. Then, as if to test the truth of the statement, he tore across the clearing and slashed at me with claws that would have shredded my chest completely . . . *if* they'd made contact.

They didn't.

Kambo staggered back again, looking at his own hands with bewildered disgust.

"You failed," I said, suddenly feeling like I was playing poker against a man with no cards. "I hope destroying me *wasn't* your Unfinished Business . . . or you're really in trouble now. How are you ever going to finish me off if you can't even *touch* me?"

I flashed a victorious smile, turned on my heel, and stopped dead.

There were two other people standing in the little glade. Well, I say *people*.

A midget with an enormous nose, shiny brass teeth, and possibly the strangest ice-cream cone haircut I have ever seen stood beside a tall, thin girl with brittle hair and a pale, blank face. One of her eyes had been sewn up, while the other gaped widely and streamed with water. She put her head to one side while the midget clasped his hands with glee.

"These are my friendsh from the brotherhood, Mishter Carble and Mish Stein. You ruined their deaths too, sho I reckonsh they might jusht wantsh to finish the job for me . . ."

I took a step back and actually passed *through* Kambo Cheapteeth.

Stein suddenly smiled and lifted off the ground, her fingers elongated and her mouth dripping with a dark red liquid that I just *knew* was blood.

Behind her, the demonic little gnome drew a strange, angular knife from his belt and crouched on the ground, proceeding toward me like a monkey on all fours.

I backed away, fast. These two new enemies both looked extremely odd, and I had a really bad feeling about fighting them.

Kambo turned to laugh as I continued to shuffle backward, trying to keep all of them in my field of vision.

The two friends of Cheapteeth had fanned out and were both stalking me from different sides—a pair of fat insects honing in on a helpless grub.

Then, for no reason that I could see, they stopped advancing . . . and Kambo's evil grin slid off his face.

Max Moon stepped out of the mist on my right, furred up and ready to fight. His jaw dripped with thick globules of saliva and his face was creased into a malicious grimace.

On my left, Jemini floated at the same height as the strange circus girl, her elongated fangs standing out like pure points of glowing light beneath the glare of the moon.

"Let's even things up a bit, shall we?" she said, aiming the remark at the clown. "You must be Kambo Cheapteeth. Evil Clive sends his regards."

For a moment, nobody moved.

Max was primed for slaughter, Jemini hovered like a wasp ready to sting, and I clenched all fourteen of my fingers . . .

. . . but Kambo's little group didn't attack.

The gnome flipped the knife back into his belt and hopped off across the field in that crouching, monkey sprint while the circus girl shot into the sky like a poisoned dart and vanished on the wind.

Kambo himself began to disappear, but slowly, as if his shadow was fading in a long drawn-out sequence.

"Thish ishn't over, Ed," came the hideous drawl. "We'll come for you again . . . when you're at your weakesht . . . when you leasht expect it."

"Not if we find you first," Jemini whispered as the clown's image flickered and faded.

Darkness settled once again on the little clearing.

LESSON 20:
ALWAYS KNOW
WHEN TO LIE

I thought my death was bad, but this was worse. I thought that being bitten by a werewolf, chased by ghouls, or choked out by my own demonic hand would have taken me to the very limits of my pain threshold . . .

. . . but I was wrong.

Thankfully, the band *did* stop playing. It just took a very long time.

I'd never been to an undead house party

before, but then I'd never been dead before, so I guess it all evened out.

The basement of Mortlake Middle School was crammed with vampires, werewolves, and assorted other creatures I couldn't even begin to describe. It seemed that every dark shadow had its own peculiar denizen of darkness, but—thankfully—I couldn't see a midget, a clown, *or* a girl with a sewn-up eye as I stared around the room.

Evil Clive's band was called Last Bus Home, for reasons I couldn't even guess at. After all, none of them would ever catch it.

As a band, they were truly awful. The guitarist had no fingers, the singer sounded like a dog with its foot caught in a bear trap, and Evil Clive would have made a better sound if he'd fallen on the drums instead of playing them . . . but we all dutifully clapped at the end (even if it was largely due to relief).

Max clapped me on the shoulder and offered me a cup of strange green liquid.

"Diet Ichor," he explained. "It's full of chemicals, but then again—you can say that about any drink that comes from a sewer . . ."

I swallowed a bit of the rancid drink and almost threw up. "Do zombies really drink this?"

Max shrugged and grinned. "Looks like you do," he said.

"You feeling any better with your old . . . er . . . *arm* back?" Jemini asked.

I nodded. "Yeah. The extra fingers are behaving a bit strangely, though."

We all glanced down at my left hand, where the extra fingers were doing their best to veer *away* from the original five.

"That's a bit weird," Jemini admitted. "Let's hope His Evil Highness can shed some light on that—shall we go sit with him for a bit?"

I nodded, thanking Max and Jemini again for saving me in the circus field. Together, the three of us meandered across the dingy, crowded dance floor toward the booth where Evil Clive and the band had set up shop.

Sure, I might stink like a fetid turkey roast, my eyeballs might be a pair of runny eggs, and the worms might actually form a union in my lower intestine, but at least I still had some idea of who I was . . . and what I was doing.

Would I ever see my family again? Would I ever get to speak—actually SPEAK, face-to-face, with Candy Lipsnicki? Sadly, I just didn't know . . .

What I DID know was that my battle with Kambo Cheapteeth had only just begun, but—for tonight, at least—I wanted to hang out with my newfound friends, and kick back and enjoy some top tunes from the new band clambering onto the stage. They were called Children of the Night . . .

. . . and their music was *sweet*.

Don't Miss

Undead Ed
and the DEMON
FREAKSHOW

read on
for a
sneak peek!

THE
DEMON ARMY

To say the demons occupied the sky in every direction would have been an understatement: they were the sky.

It took me a while to realize that each tiny gap between two demons was in fact filled . . . by at least two other demons. They were horrible, spindly, chittering humanoids with long claws, screwed up faces, and leathery wings.

The sky was heaving with them.

"We're mincemeat," Max whispered, eyeing the writhing mass of blood-red skins. "Well, I mean, you are already, but—"

"Look!"

Everyone stopped talking when Jemini pointed a shaking finger at the middle of the floating army. There, supported on a cushion of her own bizarre airstream, was Jessica Stein, Kambo Cheapteeth's demented sidekick.

I couldn't get the word *harpy* out of my head when I looked at her.

She hovered on the wind like some giant insect, hair plastered over her sallow face, and black, rotting teeth forcing her mouth into a sick smile. Her one good eye was hidden under the flow of jet locks, while its opposite continued to bleed freely from the stitches that held it firmly shut.

Thanks to Jemini's brilliant research skills, we now knew a lot more about Miss Stein than we had when I first ran into her. A tightrope walker with a love of unspeakable heights, she'd been committed to a lunatic asylum when she went wild during a show and started to randomly attack the audience. Before the police could capture her, however, she'd broken into a shop that sold doll's houses and sewn one of her own eyelids shut. No one knew why.

What we did know was that in death she could float unaided and had claws like a dragon.

"Run!" Forgoth shouted, shaking me from my reverie. "Run!"

"NO! STAND YOUR GROUND! THEY WILL NOT ENTER THIS HOUSE!" Mrs. Looker cried, throwing out her hands in a wild gesture. All the doors and windows slammed shut, some with such force that a line of terrible cracks appeared in the plaster. The house on Prospect Hill had sealed like Fort Knox in a matter of seconds.

I would have been well impressed had it not been for the fact that we were watching the sky through a hole in the living room wall.

We didn't get much time to dwell on this, as it was at that precise moment that the demons fell on us like a rogue wave in a surfing competition, breaking over the house in their hundreds.

The two werewolves immediately took to

their heels, furring up and howling like the wind as they exploded from the house and tore into the demons.

Half-submerged in the throes of change, both werewolves hit the demon swarm with a bang. Two of the hideous creatures immediately flew back into the air, somersaulting over each other and screaming in frustrated anger at the strength of the frenzied attack. But victory for the pair was short lived: two demons cast aside became four swooping back, three ripped apart became six fresh and ready to bite.

"They can't enter the house," Jemini whispered excitedly, as several of the gangly creatures dived for the gap in the wall only to recoil as if they'd flown into a hot griddle. "It's Mrs. Looker—she's done something to the boundaries."

"They're two of my pack," Max growled, his teeth and fingernails beginning to lengthen. "And they're not at their strongest without moonlight. I can't just stand here with you guys and watch them shredded in front of me."

"Maximus Moon," Jemini said, turning to glare at him. "Don't you DARE go out there."

But she was talking to dead air: the wolf leapt through the hole and tore to the defense of his friends, just as another batch of demons lunged out of the sky.

"Max!" Jemini screamed, leaning out of the opening in the brickwork and making frantic gestures with her arms. "Max!"

Blue coils of electricity covered the holes

in the house like fishing nets, repelling the demons at every point. Mrs. Looker was muttering under her breath, snakes of energy crackling from her hands and feet as her eyes rolled back inside her head. As a further raft of electric tendrils danced from her shoulders and sizzled all over the house, she snatched hold of Forgoth, preventing the little phantom from leaving the house. More and more demons were flocking to attack Max Moon, and I watched with mounting horror as he reared and struck out in full werewolf form, sending several of the fiends somersaulting backward amid spiraling sprays of their own glistening green blood.

Well done, Ed. The voice cackled inside my head, and it had an edge to it. I couldn't tell if it was my own voice or the voice of Kambo that had dwelled in my hand . . . or even some strange mixture of the two, but it was definitely talking to me. *That's the spirit. Watch your friends suffer and die while you're safe on the inside, protected, coddled, safeguarded by the old witch woman. There's a word for what you are, Ed—a word that sums up exactly what you're all about.*

COWARD.

Max was losing the fight. Max Moon, my first real friend in the world of the dead, was being forced to his knees by the demon horde, while their cackling and demented ghoul of a leader hovered in the sky and clapped her hands with unconcealed glee.

COWARD.

Mrs. Looker threw me a warning glance,

but she'd have needed an army to stop me from hitting the hillside.

I might be a pathetic, putrid, stinking zombie, and I might be losing more and more flesh by the day . . . but I was still possessed of a limb that had single-handedly eviscerated packs of ghouls and an entire clan of revenants. It was time to fight.